花馬

Huā Mǎ

In Search of Hua Ma

John Pasden and Jared Turner

Chinese Graded Readers

Published by Mind Spark Press LLC Shanghai, China

Mandarin Companion is a trademark of Mind Spark Press LLC.

Copyright © Mind Spark Press LLC, 2019

For information about educational or bulk purchases, please contact Mind Spark Press at BUSINESS@MANDARINCOMPANION.COM.

Instructor and learner resources and traditional Chinese editions of the Mandarin Companion series are available at
WWW.MANDARINCOMPANION.COM.

First paperback print edition 2019

Library of Congress Cataloging-in-Publication Data In Search of Hua Ma: Mandarin Companion Graded Readers: Breakthrough Level, Simplified Chinese Edition / John Pasden and Jared Turner; [edited by] John Pasden, Chen Shishuang, Li Jiong, Ma Lihua Shanghai, China: Mind Spark Press LLC, 2019 Library of Congress Control Number: 2019948191

ISBN: 9781941875537 (Paperback)
ISBN: 9781941875551 (Paperback/traditional ch)
ISBN: 9781941875544 (ebook)
ISBN: 9781941875568 (ebook/traditional ch)

MCID: TFH20220818T091759

All rights reserved; no part of this publication may be reproduced, stored in a retrieval system, transmitted in any form, or by any means, electronic, mechanical, photocopying, recording, or otherwise, without the prior written permission of the publishers.

What Graded Readers can do for you

Welcome to Mandarin Companion!

We've worked hard to create enjoyable stories that can help you build confidence and competence and get better at Chinese–at the right level for you.

Our graded readers have controlled and simplified language that allows you to bring together the language you've learned so far and absorb how words work naturally together. Research suggests that learners need to "encounter" a word 10-30 times before truly learning it. Graded readers provide the repetition that you need to develop fluency NOW at your level.

In the next section, you can take an assessment and discover if this is the right level for you. We also explain how it won't just improve your Chinese skills but will have a wide range of benefits, from better test scores to increased confidence.

We hope you enjoy our books, and best of luck with your studies. Jared and John

Frequently Asked Questions

Do you have versions with pinyin over the characters?

No. Although this method is common for native Chinese learners, research and experience show it distracts a second language learner and slows down their ability to learn the characters. If you require pinyin to read most of the characters at this level, you should read something easier.

Is there an English translation of the story?

No. Research and experience show that an English translation will slow down the development of your Chinese language learning skills.

Is this the right level for me?

Let's find out. Open to a story page with characters and start reading. Keep track of the number of characters you *don't* know but don't count any key words you don't know. If there are more than 5 unknown characters on that page, you may want to consider working on your basic character recognition before attempting a graded reader. If the unknown characters are fewer than 5, then this book is likely at your level! If you find that you know all the characters, you may be ready for a higher level. However, even if you know all the characters but are reading slowly, you should consider building reading speed before moving up a level.

How do you decide which characters to include at each level?

Each level includes a core set of characters based on our extensive analysis of the most common characters and words taught to and used by those learning Chinese as a second language. All books at each level are based on the same core set and they can be read in any order.

What to expect in a Breakthrough book?

It's important that you read at the level that is right for you. Check out the next page to learn more about Extensive Reading and how we use that in graded readers to support the learning of Chinese by just enjoying a good story.

Books in our Breakthrough Level like this one:

- Include a core set of 150 Chinese words and characters learners are most likely to know.
- Are about 5,000 characters in length
- Use level appropriate grammar

- Include pinyin and a translation of words and characters you are not expected to know at this level
- Include a glossary at the back of book
- Include proper nouns that are underlined

What is Extensive Reading?

It will improve test scores, your reading speed and comprehension, speaking, listening and writing skills. You'll pick up grammar naturally, you'll begin understanding in Chinese, your confidence will improve, and you'll enjoy learning the language.

Graded Readers are based on science that is backed by mountains of research and proven by learners all over the world. They are founded on the theories of Extensive Reading and Comprehensible Input.

Extensive Reading is reading at a level where you can understand almost all of what you are reading (ideally 98%) at a comfortable speed, as opposed to stumbling through dense paragraphs word by word.

When you read extensively, you'll understand most of the words and find yourself fully engaged with the story.

Reading at 98% comprehension is the sweet spot to max out your learning gains. You do still learn at the Intensive Reading level (90–98%), but the closer you are to the Extensive level, the faster your progress.

No one should be reading below a 90% comprehension level.

It's called Reading Pain for a reason. You spend so much time in a dictionary and after 30 painful minutes on ONE paragraph, you're not even sure what you've just read!

If you want to know more, check out our website
www.mandarincompanion.com

Table of Contents

Story Notes — vii
Character Adaptations — viii
Cast of Characters — viii
Locations — x

Chapter 1 去山上找花 — 1
Chapter 2 看見了一個老太太 — 6
Chapter 3 到海南了? — 11
Chapter 4 找花馬 — 16
Chapter 5 頭上有花的馬 — 22
Chapter 6 老人 — 26
Chapter 7 老人知道了 — 32
Chapter 8 真的花馬 — 38
Chapter 9 回山西 — 44
Chapter 10 媽媽很開心 — 51

Key Words — 55
Grammar Points — 59
Credits and Acknowledgments — 62
About Mandarin Companion — 63
Other Stories from Mandarin Companion — 64

Story Notes

The Mandarin Companion 150-character Breakthrough Level empowers Chinese learners to begin with positive and enjoyable experiences reading Chinese. For learners at this level, reading a book in Chinese provides both a boost in fluency and a sense of accomplishment. Differing from higher level stories in the series, these are original stories co-written by John Pasden and Jared Turner, specifically designed to engage readers despite the limitations.

Stories at the Breakthrough Level are unique, with all books limited to the same small set of 150 characters comprising nouns, verbs and adjectives repeated throughout the books. Keywords are selectively borrowed from within the Mandarin Companion Level 1 standard. Those who can read this book at an enjoyable pace are already well on their way towards reading Mandarin Companion Level 1 stories.

In Search of Hua Ma is one of our more fantastical stories, partly inspired by books like *Alice in Wonderland* and *The Lion, the Witch, and the Wardrobe*. However, this story also ties into the larger "Mandarin Companion Universe." Continue reading other Mandarin Companion stories and you'll find a character from this story in *The 60-Year Dream*, a Mandarin Companion Level 1 story.

Character Adaptations

The following is a list of the characters from this Chinese story followed by their corresponding English names from John Pasden and Jared Turner's original story. The names below are not translations; they are new Chinese names used for the Chinese versions of the original characters. Think of them as all-new characters in a Chinese story.

南南 (Nánnán) – Nannan
媽媽 (Nánnán Māma) – Nannan's Mom
老太太 (Lǎo Tàitai) – Old Woman
老頭 (Lǎotóu) – Old Man
花馬 (Huā Mǎ) – Hua Ma

Cast of Characters

南南
(Nánnán)

媽媽
(Nánnán Māma)

老太太
(Lǎo Tàitai)

老頭
(Lǎotóu)

花馬
(Huā Mǎ)

Locations

山西 (Shānxī)

Shanxi Province in northern China (not to be confused with Shaanxi 陕西), meaning "West of the Mountains", is characterized by arid plateaus surrounded by mountain ranges.

海南 (Hǎinán)

The southernmost province of China, Hainan is a large tropical island off the southern coast of mainland China. Today it is known as a popular tourist destination for its clear water and white sandy beaches.

去山上找花

山西有很多山，很多山西人都住在山上。南南和他的爸爸媽媽也住在山西的一個山上。

南南每天都去山上玩，因為山上有很多很好玩的地方。山上也有一些花，可是都很小，也不是很好看。

---

1 住在 (zhù zài) *vc.* to live (in/at)
2 山上 (shānshàng) *phrase* on the mountain(s)
3 因為 (yīnwèi) *conj.* because
4 好玩 (hǎowán) *adj.* fun
5 地方 (dìfang) *n.* place
6 一些 (yīxiē) *n.* some
7 可是 (kěshì) *conj.* but
8 好看 (hǎokàn) *adj.* good-looking

山上的人沒有很多錢，可是，大家還是很開心。

一天早上，南南聽爸爸說，媽媽的生日快到了。他很開心，他要在媽

9　大家 (dàjiā) *n.* everyone
10　還是 (háishi) *conj., adv.* still
11　開心 (kāixīn) *adj.* happy
12　早上 (zǎoshang) *tn.* morning
13　聽 (tīng) *v.* to listen (to)
14　生日 (shēngrì) *n.* birthday

媽生日那天給她一個東西。因為每年南南生日的時候,媽媽都有東西給他。那些東西都不用花很多錢,可是,南南很開心。

南南想:"我給媽媽什麼東西呢?"他沒有錢。他要的東西,爸爸媽媽會給他。可是,他們不會給他錢。

"怎麼做呢?什麼東西又好看,又不花錢?"南南在山上一邊走,一邊看。

15	那天 (nà tiān) *tn.* that day
16	東西 (dōngxi) *n.* thing(s), stuff
17	每年 (měi nián) *phrase* every year
18	的時候 (de shíhou) *phrase* when…
19	怎麼 (zěnme) *adv.* how
20	又 (yòu) *adv.* again
21	花錢 (huā qián) *vo.* to spend money
22	一邊 (yībiān) *conj.* while doing… (two things)

"有了!"南南開心地說。

回到家,媽媽問:"南南,你怎麼這麼開心?"

"這個還不能說。可是,你會知道的。"南南開心地說。

23 開心地 (kāixīn de) *phrase* happily
24 家 (jiā) *n.* home
25 這麼 (zhème) *adv.* so…
26 還 (hái) *adv.* still
27 第二天 (dì-èr tiān) *phrase* the next day

第二天,南南一個人去山上找花。山上的花不多,南南一個人找了很長時間,還是沒找到很好看的花。

不知道走了多長時間,南南看到了一個小房子。這個地方他沒來過。

"這個房子這麼老,誰會住在這個地方呢?"

---

28 一個人 (yī gè rén) *phrase* alone
29 找 (zhǎo) *v.* to look for
30 時間 (shíjiān) *n.* time
31 多長時間 (duō cháng shíjiān) *phrase* how long (of a time)
32 看到 (kàndào) *vc.* to see
33 房子 (fángzi) *n.* house

Two

看見了一個老太太

南南走到門邊問："裡面有人嗎？"沒有人給他開門。南南看到門沒有關，開門走了進去。

"你找誰？"一個很老的老太太走出來對南南說。

"老太太，你好，我叫南南。我在山

---

34 門邊 (mén biān) *phrase* by the door
35 裡面 (lǐmiàn) *n.* inside
36 開門 (kāimén) *vo.* to open the door
37 進去 (jìnqu) *vc.* to go in
38 老太太 (lǎotàitai) *n.* old lady
39 走出來 (zǒu chūlai) *vc.* to walk out (from)
40 叫 (jiào) *v.* to be called, to call; to tell (someone to do something)

上走了很長時間,不知道怎麼走到了這裡,也不知道要怎麼回家。"

"你為什麼在山上走很長時間?你要找什麼?"老太太問。

"又大又好看的花。明天是媽媽

的生日，可是，我沒有錢。只能來山上找花。"南南看看老太太，又說："我每天都去山上玩，我知道山上有一些小花，可是，我找不到又大又好看的花。"

"南南，你說你每天都去山上玩。你在山上有沒有見過'花馬'"？老太太問。

"什麼'馬'？"南南問。

"'花馬'。"老太太又說了一次。

42 只能 (zhǐnéng) adv. can only
43 看看 (kànkan) v. to take a look
44 找不到 (zhǎo bu dào) vc. to be unable to find
45 見過 (jiàn guo) phrase have met before
46 一次 (yīcì) phrase one time

"我不知道你說的是什麼馬。"南南說,"可是,我在山上沒見過馬。"

"我要你去找'花馬'。"

"可是,我都說了,山上什麼馬都沒有。"南南想老太太沒聽見。

"南南,要是找不到'花馬',你不能回家。"老太太笑了笑,"要是你找到了,你可以回家,我也會給你又大又好看的花。"

"我要回家!因為明天是我媽媽

---

47 聽見 (tīngjiàn) *vc.* to hear
48 要是 (yàoshi) *conj.* if
49 笑 (xiào) *v.* to laugh, to smile

的生日,我沒有時間找你的馬。"南南一邊說,一邊走出老太太的家。

到海南了？

"這是什麼地方……？"南南出門以後，看到了大海。

"這是哪兒？怎麼會有大海？那些山去哪兒了？我在哪兒？"南南不知道問誰，因為他一個人也看不到。

"這不是真的吧，我在哪兒……"

---

51 出門 (chūmén) *vo.* to go out the door, to go outside
52 以後 (yǐhòu) *adv.* after; later, in the future
53 大海 (dàhǎi) *n.* the ocean
54 怎麼會 (zěnme huì) *phrase* how could
55 看不到 (kàn bu dào) *vc.* to be unable to see
56 真的 (zhēn de) *adj., adv.* real; really

他回頭去開老太太家的門，可是，老太太的家和那個老太太都不見了。

"怎麼會這樣……"南南很怕，他不知道這是哪兒，他也不知道怎麼做。

他在海邊一邊走，一邊看。他看到地上的字：海南。

"我在海南？我怎麼會從山西到了海南……"

"這裡的海真好看！"南南看看大海，

57	回頭 (huítóu) *vo.* to turn one's head	60	怕 (pà) *v.* to be afraid (of)
58	不見了 (bùjiàn le) *phrase* disappeared	61	海邊 (hǎibiān) *n.* seaside
59	這樣 (zhèyàng) *pr.* like this	62	地上 (dìshang) *n.* on the ground

這是他第一次看到這麼好看的海。

南南從小到大都在山西。他沒有去過山西外面的地方。

海南的 天、大海都 很好看。可是,

63 第一次 (dì-yī cì) *phrase* first time
64 從小到大 (cóng xiǎo dào dà) *phrase* from a young age until adulthood
65 外面 (wàimian) *n.* outside

明天是媽媽的生日，南南要回山西的家。

"花馬，花馬，你在哪兒？"南南一邊走，一邊叫。南南想："'花馬'是馬的名字嗎？"

南南想："老太太說我要去找她的馬。可是，她也不說怎麼找，我也不知道怎麼找。"

在海邊又走了一會兒，南南還是沒有看到馬。

---

66 名字 (míngzi) *n.* name　　67 一會兒 (yīhuìr) *tn.* a little while

他不走了，對大海大叫："花馬，你在哪兒？花馬，我是南南，我是來找你的，你出來吧，跟我回家吧……"

說到這裡，南南不說了，他想：花馬是馬，馬怎麼可能知道有人在找它……

這時候，他聽到有人在說話。他看到了他們，那些人看起來很小，都沒有南南大。

---

68 **大叫** (dà jiào) *v.* to call out loudly
69 **出來** (chūlai) *vc.* to come out
70 **可能** (kěnéng) *adv.; aux* maybe, possibly; possible
71 **這時候** (zhè shíhou) *phrase* at this time
72 **聽到** (tīngdào) *vc.* to hear
73 **說話** (shuōhuà) *vo.* to speak (words), to talk
74 **看起來** (kàn qǐlai) *vc.* to look...

找花馬

"你們好。"南南說,"我叫南南,這裡真的是海南嗎?你們是海南人嗎?你們在這裡做什麼?"

"對,我們是海南人。我們是這裡的工人。"一個人說。

"我是從山西來的。"南南說,"你們這裡有馬嗎?我是來找馬的。"

工人 (gōngrén) *n.* worker

"你要找什麼馬?"一個工人問。

"我今天在山上見到一個老太太,老太太說我找一個'花馬'。"

"我們這裡只有花,沒有馬。"一個工人笑了,"你看,那邊有很多又大又好看的花。"

南南看了一下："真好看！我也在給我媽媽找花！可是，我要找的是'花馬'，有人聽說過它的名字嗎？"

聽他說完，大家都笑了。可是，他們只笑，不說。

南南說："我從小到大都沒見過馬，你們見過嗎？"

"你為什麼要找'花馬'？你是馬媽媽嗎？"一個工人問。大家聽了以後

77　一下 (yīxià)　adv.　briefly, for a second
78　聽說 (tīngshuō)　v.　to hear tell, to hear said (that)
79　說完 (shuō wán)　vc.　to finish speaking

都在笑。

"什麼馬媽媽?"南南有一點生氣了。"'花馬'是馬,對嗎?我怎麼會是它的媽媽?"

"你看,這裡都是海,你要找的馬會不會在海裡呢?"一個人問南南。

大家還在笑。

南南看看海,又看看這些人,有一點生氣地說:"馬怎麼可能住在海裡?"

"誰說海裡沒有馬?"一個工人

---

80 有一點 (yǒu yīdiǎn) *phrase* to be a little (too)

81 生氣 (shēngqì) *vo., adj.* to get angry; angry

82 生氣地 (shēngqì de) *phrase* angrily

有一點生氣,大叫,"你沒聽說過海馬嗎?"

大家又笑。

"海馬是海馬,不是我要找的馬。我要找真的馬!"南南也大叫。南南又說:"我看,你們都不知道'花馬'。好吧,我一個人去找。這個地方這麼大,我要怎麼走呢?"

"你看,那邊有個小房子。"一個好心的工人說,"去那邊吧。"

"謝謝。"南南對工人們說,"我走了。再見。"

---

84 好心的 (hǎoxīn de) *adj.* kind-hearted

Five

頭上有花的馬

海南每個地方都有很多好看的花。

南南一邊走一邊看花。

"那是什麼?"南南看到一個很大的東西。可是,他看不到它的頭。

南南小心地走了過去:"花馬?!"

他大叫,"是你嗎,花馬?你是花馬,對不對?"

---

85 小心地 (xiǎoxīn de) *phrase* carefully   86 過去 (guòqu) *vc.* to go over

南南很開心,因為這是馬,它頭上還有一個很大的"花"字。

馬看看南南,點了一下頭。

"太好了!我找到了!我找到花馬了!"南南說,"花馬,你知道不知道

---

87 點了一下頭 (diǎn le yīxià tóu) *phrase* to nod briefly

有人在找你，跟我回家吧。"

馬點了一下頭，跟南南走了。

"花馬，我真怕找不到你。"南南笑了一下，他很開心地說："你知道我在找你，對不對？"

馬點了一下頭。

"你真是好馬！回家以後，我們一起去山上玩，好不好？"

馬又點了一下頭，可是，它不跟南南走了。

---

88 一起 (yīqǐ) *adv.* together

"不對,花馬,不是那邊,是這邊。跟我走,好不好?"南南大叫。

馬點了一下頭,可是,它還是不聽南南的話,也不跟他走。

老人

"花馬,你怎麼了?怎麼又對我點頭,又不聽我的話呢?"南南看起來有一點生氣。

馬又對南南點了一下頭。

南南想:"花馬怎麼會這樣?我說什麼它都點頭,這不對吧……它是真的花馬嗎……?"

---

89 怎麼了 (zěnme le) *phrase* what happened, what's the matter

90 點頭 (diǎntóu) *vo.* to nod one's head

馬看了看大海，走了。

"花馬，你去哪兒？這裡是海南，我們的家在山西。跟我走吧。"南南一邊走一邊說。可是，馬不跟南南走，南南也不知道怎麼做，他想了想，跟馬走了。

馬走到一個小房子門邊，不走了。

"花馬，這是哪兒？"南南走到門邊問："有人嗎？"

開門的是一個很老很老的老頭。他

---

91 想了想 (xiǎng le xiǎng) *phrase* thought about it for a second

92 老頭 (lǎotóu) *n.* old man

問南南："你找誰？"

南南看了看說："老先生，你好。我叫南南，我是跟花馬來你家的。"南南問老人，"這是你的馬吧？"

---

93 老先生 (lǎo xiānsheng) *phrase* elderly gentleman

94 老人 (lǎorén) *n.* old person, old man

老頭說:"什麼花馬?我不知道這是誰的馬。"

南南說:"老先生,你家裡還有人嗎?我來問問你家人吧,他們可能知道花馬是誰的。"

"家人?這裡只有我。你知道我是誰嗎?"老人問。

南南說:"不知道。你叫什麼?。"

"我叫什麼……問得好,我也不知道我叫什麼。"

---

95 家人 (jiārén) *n.* family member(s)

96 問得好 (wèn de hǎo) *phrase* good question (lit. "well asked")

"老先生,花馬來找你,你真的不知道花馬嗎?"南南又問,"它來找你,可能因為你們是朋友。"

老頭說:"我一個人住在這裡,沒有朋友。"

"不會吧？你在這裡住了多長時間了？"南南又問。

"我不知道。你不要問我了，我什麼都不知道。你走吧。"老人要關門了。

---

97 關門 (guānmén) *vo.* to close a door

Seven

老人知道了

南南說:"老先生,你不要關門。你聽我說完,可以嗎?"

老人看看南南說:"好吧,你進來吧。"

南南說:"在山西的一個山上,有一個老太太,跟你一樣老。她叫我來找花馬。我找到了這個馬,它頭上也有

98　進來 (jìnlai)　*v.* to come in　　99　一樣 (yīyàng)　*n.* the same

一個'花'字。可是,我也不知道它是不是花馬。"

"那你問問這個馬。"老人說。他笑了一下。

"我問過了,可是我問什麼,它都會點頭,我怎麼知道是不是真的……"南南說完,看看馬,問:"花馬,這個老人是你的朋友嗎?"

馬看看老人,點了一下頭。

南南看看馬,又問:"花馬,你頭上的'花'字是這個老人寫的嗎?"

馬看看老人,又點了一下頭,大叫了一下。

南南聽了有一點怕,因為他想這馬只會點頭。

"看起來,這馬不是隻會點頭。"

老人笑了。

南南看老人笑了，又不怕了。南南問："老先生，是真的嗎？這個'花'字是你寫的嗎？"

老人沒聽南南說話,他一邊看馬,一邊說："花，馬，花，馬，花……"

南南不知道老人怎麼了,只能問馬:"花馬，你知道嗎？你真的知道我在問什麼嗎？"

馬沒點頭，也沒叫。

這時候，老人笑了："不對，它不

是花馬，花馬不是馬。」

"什麼？你說什麼？"南南說，"你再說一次……"

"花馬是我，不是它。"老人又說。

南南說："可是，你是人，你不是馬。花馬怎麼會是人……你說的不是真的！"

---

100 再 (zài) *adv.* again (in the future)

Eight

真的花馬

"我說的是真的。'花馬'真的是我的名字，不是馬的名字。"老人看看馬，笑了一下。

南南說："怎麼會這樣……那，這馬是不是你的馬？"

老頭說："是我的馬。"

"那，馬頭上的這個'花'字，也

是你寫的?"南南開心地問。

"對。我在它頭上寫這個'花'字,因為我的名字是花馬。"老人很開心,因為他知道自己是誰了,他還找到了他的馬。"你知道嗎?這馬也很老了,它沒有我老,可是,我們是真的老朋友了。"

馬點了一下頭。

"真好!"南南開心地說,"我太開心了!我找到了你,你找到了你的老

朋友。我們可以回去了!老太太見到你,會很開心的!"

"什麼老太太?"老人問,"她是誰?為什麼她見到我會開心?"

"我也不知道那個老太太是誰,我

---

101 回去 (huíqu) *vc.* to go back

和她也是第一次見面。她住在山上一個很老的房子裡。"

"那，我們去她家看看吧，可能我知道她是誰。"老人說。

"可是，我也不知道我們要怎麼回去……出了她的家以後，我看到的是大海，山都沒了……我不知道我在哪兒，我回頭看的時候，老太太的家不見了，她也不見了。"

---

102 見面 (jiànmiàn) *vo.* to meet

"那,我們能不能一起回去找一找?"老人問。

"可以,我知道那個地方的地上寫了'海南'。那裡可能有門。跟我走吧!"南南說。

"還有你。"南南看了看馬。

馬點了一下頭,老人和南南一起笑了笑。

Nine

回山西

"我們到了!"南南很開心,"可是那個門,在哪裡?"

老人說:"我知道這個地方。"

南南說:"門呢?"

老人笑了笑說:"你看,這不是門嗎?"

南南看了看,真的有門了。"有門

了！怎麼會？"南南說。真的是老太太家的門。

"太好了，那我們進去看看吧。"老人對南南笑笑。馬也點了一下頭。

南南有一點怕，"我要回家，我要回家！可是，這樣能回去嗎？"

"你不進去也可以，你要一個人在這裡嗎？"老人笑了笑問。

"我不要一個人在這裡……"南南叫，"我還是跟你們一起進去吧。"

說完，老人開了門，他們一起進去了。

他們看到了老太太。南南開心地說："花馬，你看！是那個老太太，我們回來了！"

"花馬，是你嗎？他真的找到你了！"老太太看到老人和馬，開心地笑了笑。她走過來，說："花馬，你回家了。"

"是我，我回來了。對不起，我不會再走了。"

---

103 回來 (huílai) vc. to come back
104 走過來 (zǒu guòlai) vc. to walk over
105 對不起 (duìbuqǐ) phrase I'm sorry

"你們是?"南南看看他們,問:"這裡是你們的家?"

"對,我們在這裡一起住了很多年。"老人說,"可是,我走了。我走了以後我不知道我是誰,我在哪兒。現在我知道了,我回來了。"

"一百年了……我們一百年沒見面了……"老太太說。

"真的一百年了嗎?對不起,我不會再走了。"花馬說。

馬點了一下頭。

"老太太,我找到了花馬,可以回家了吧?"南南問老太太。

"明天是你媽媽的生日,我說過我會給你一些又大又好看的花。"老太

太笑笑說,"你看,這些花都是給你媽媽的。好看嗎?"

"真好看!"南南笑了,"山西沒有這麼好看的花。我在山上也沒找到這麼好看的花。"

"謝謝你,老太太。我回家了。"南南一邊說一邊走,走到門邊,看了看老太太,又說"這是我回家的門嗎?"

"是回家的門,南南。謝謝你!再見。"老太太說完,關上了門。

南南出了門,又回頭看了看老太太的家。可是,老太太的房子……又不見了!

可是,他看到了很多山,他知道山上有他的家。

媽媽很開心

"爸爸媽媽,我回來了!"回到家,南南很開心。

"南南,你去哪兒了?怎麼這麼開心?"媽媽一邊和南南說話,一邊做明天生日的飯。

"媽媽,我有好東西要給你。"南南笑笑說。

"什麼好東西？"媽媽也笑。

"你看！"南南說，手裡都是花。"爸爸，你也過來看看。"

"這麼大的花？！山上有嗎？你在哪兒找到的？"爸爸問。"真好看！"

南南沒說話，只笑了一下，說："媽媽，明天是你的生日，這些花是給你的。你開心嗎？"

"謝謝兒子，媽媽很開心。"媽媽笑得很好看。

---

107 手裡 (shǒu lǐ) *phrase* in one's hand
108 過來 (guòlai) *vc.* to come over
109 兒子 (érzi) *n.* son

"媽媽,看到你這麼開心,我也很開心。"南南說。

"兒子,我從小到大都沒見過這麼好看的花。"

媽媽看看花,又問:"南南,媽媽知道,我們這裡沒有這麼好看的山花。

媽媽要問你，這些花是哪裡來的？"

"是一個朋友給我的。"南南有一點怕，爸爸媽媽都不知道他今天去找"花馬"了。要是他們知道了，可能以後他都不可以再去山上玩了。

媽媽問："這個朋友是老太太嗎？"

南南說："媽媽，你怎麼知道？"

媽媽看了看爸爸，笑了。

Key Words 關鍵詞 (Guānjiàncí)

1. 住在 zhù zài *vc.* to live (in/at)
2. 山上 shānshàng *phrase* on the mountain(s)
3. 因為 yīnwèi *conj.* because
4. 好玩 hǎowán *adj.* fun
5. 地方 dìfang *n.* place
6. 一些 yīxiē *n.* some
7. 可是 kěshì *conj.* but
8. 好看 hǎokàn *adj.* good-looking
9. 大家 dàjiā *n.* everyone
10. 還是 háishi *conj., adv.* still
11. 開心 kāixīn *adj.* happy
12. 早上 zǎoshang *tn.* morning
13. 聽 tīng *v.* to listen (to)
14. 生日 shēngrì *n.* birthday
15. 那天 nà tiān *tn.* that day
16. 東西 dōngxi *n.* thing(s), stuff
17. 每年 měi nián *phrase* every year
18. 的時候 de shíhou *phrase* when…
19. 怎麼 zěnme *adv.* how
20. 又 yòu *adv.* again
21. 花錢 huā qián *vo.* to spend money
22. 一邊 yībiān *conj.* while doing… (two things)
23. 開心地 kāixīn de *phrase* happily
24. 家 jiā *n.* home
25. 這麼 zhème *adv.* so…
26. 還 hái *adv.* still

27. 第二天 dì-èr tiān *phrase* the next day
28. 一個人 yī gè rén *phrase* alone
29. 找 zhǎo *v.* to look for
30. 時間 shíjiān *n.* time
31. 多長時間 duō cháng shíjiān *phrase* how long (of a time)
32. 看到 kàndào *vc.* to see
33. 房子 fángzi *n.* house
34. 門邊 mén biān *phrase* by the door
35. 裡面 lǐmiàn *n.* inside
36. 開門 kāimén *vo.* to open the door
37. 進去 jìnqu *vc.* to go in
38. 老太太 lǎotàitai *n.* old lady
39. 走出來 zǒu chūlai *vc.* to walk out (from)
40. 叫 jiào *v.* to be called, to call; to tell (someone to do something)
41. 回家 huíjiā *vo.* to go home
42. 只能 zhǐnéng *adv.* can only
43. 看看 kànkan *v.* to take a look
44. 找不到 zhǎo bu dào *vc.* to be unable to find
45. 見過 jiàn guo *phrase* have met before
46. 一次 yīcì *phrase* one time
47. 聽見 tīngjiàn *vc.* to hear
48. 要是 yàoshi *conj.* if
49. 笑 xiào *v.* to laugh, to smile
50. 走出 zǒuchū *vc.* to walk out
51. 出門 chūmén *vo.* to go out the door, to go outside
52. 以後 yǐhòu *adv.* after; later, in the future
53. 大海 dàhǎi *n.* the ocean
54. 怎麼會 zěnme huì *phrase* how could
55. 看不到 kàn bu dào *vc.* to be unable to see
56. 真的 zhēn de *adj., adv.* real; really
57. 回頭 huítóu *vo.* to turn one's head
58. 不見了 bùjiàn le *phrase* disappeared
59. 這樣 zhèyàng *pr.* like this
60. 怕 pà *v.* to be afraid (of)
61. 海邊 hǎibiān *n.* seaside

62. 地上 dìshang *n.* on the ground
63. 第一次 dì-yī cì *phrase* first time
64. 從小到大 cóng xiǎo dào dà *phrase* from a young age until adulthood
65. 外面 wàimian *n.* outside
66. 名字 míngzi *n.* name
67. 一會兒 yīhuìr *tn.* a little while
68. 大叫 dà jiào *v.* to call out loudly
69. 出來 chūlai *vc.* to come out
70. 可能 kěnéng *adv.; aux* maybe, possibly; possible
71. 這時候 zhè shíhou *phrase* at this time
72. 聽到 tīngdào *vc.* to hear
73. 說話 shuōhuà *vo.* to speak (words), to talk
74. 看起來 kàn qǐlai *vc.* to look...
75. 工人 gōngrén *n.* worker
76. 那邊 nàbiān *n.* over there
77. 一下 yīxià *adv.* briefly, for a second
78. 聽說 tīngshuō *v.* to hear tell, to hear said (that)
79. 說完 shuō wán *vc.* to finish speaking
80. 有一點 yǒu yīdiǎn *phrase* to be a little (too)
81. 生氣 shēngqì *vo., adj.* to get angry; angry
82. 生氣地 shēngqì de *phrase* angrily
83. 海馬 hǎimǎ *n.* seahorse
84. 好心的 hǎoxīn de *adj.* kind-hearted
85. 小心地 xiǎoxīn de *phrase* carefully
86. 過去 guòqu *vc.* to go over
87. 點了一下頭 diǎn le yīxià tóu *phrase* to nod briefly
88. 一起 yīqǐ *adv.* together
89. 怎麼了 zěnme le *phrase* what happened, what's the matter
90. 點頭 diǎntóu *vo.* to nod one's head
91. 想了想 xiǎng le xiǎng *phrase* thought about it for a second
92. 老頭 lǎotóu *n.* old man
93. 老先生 lǎo xiānsheng *phrase* elderly gentleman
94. 老人 lǎorén *n.* old person, old man
95. 家人 jiārén *n.* family member(s)
96. 問得好 wèn de hǎo *phrase* good question (lit. "well asked")

97. 關門 guānmén *vo.* to close a door
98. 進來 jìnlai *v.* to come in
99. 一樣 yīyàng *n.* the same
100. 再 zài *adv.* again (in the future)
101. 回去 huíqu *vc.* to go back
102. 見面 jiànmiàn *vo.* to meet
103. 回來 huílai *vc.* to come back
104. 走過來 zǒu guòlai *vc.* to walk over
105. 對不起 duìbuqǐ *phrase* I'm sorry
106. 一百年 yībǎi nián *phrase* 100 years
107. 手裡 shǒu lǐ *phrase* in one's hand
108. 過來 guòlai *vc.* to come over
109. 兒子 érzi *n.* son

Part of Speech Key

adj. Adjective
adv. Adverb
aux. Auxiliary Verb
conj. Conjunction
cov. Coverb
mw. Measure word
n. Noun
on. Onomatopoeia
part. Particle

prep. Preposition
pr. Pronoun
pn. Proper noun
tn. Time Noun
v. Verb
vc. Verb plus complement
vo. Verb plus object

Grammar Points

For learners new to reading Chinese, an understanding of grammar points can be extremely helpful for learners and teachers. The following is a list of the most challenging grammar points used in this graded reader.

These grammar points correspond to the Common European Framework of Reference for Languages (CEFR) level A2 or above. The full list with explanations and examples of each grammar point can be found on the Chinese Grammar Wiki, the definitive source of information on Chinese grammar online.

ENGLISH	CHINESE
CHAPTER 1	
Special cases of "zai" following verbs	Verb + 在 + Place
The "also" adverb "ye"	也 + Verb / Adj.
Cause and effect with "yinwei" and "suoyi"	因為……所以……
Expressing "when" with "de shihou"	……的時候
Expressing "together" with "yiqi"	一起 + Verb
Two words for "but"	……，可是 / 但是……
Degree complement	Verb + 得……
Questions with "ne"	……呢?
Expressing "both A and B" with "you"	又……又……
Simultaneous tasks with "yibian"	一邊 + Verb 1 (,) 一邊 + Verb 2
Ordinal numbers with "di"	第 + Number (+ Measure Word)

Asking why with "zenme"	怎麼……?
Adjectives with "name" and "zheme"	那麼 / 這麼 + Adj.
Indicating a number in excess	Number + 多
Expressing experiences with "guo"	Verb + 過

CHAPTER 2

A softer "but" with "buguo"	……, 不過……

CHAPTER 3

After a specific time with "yihou"	Time / Verb + 以後
Expressing "from…to…" with "cong…dao…"	從……到……
Expressing "really" with "zhen"	真 + Adj.
Reduplication of verbs	Verb + Verb
How to do something with "zenme"	怎麼 + Verb ?
Direction complement	Verb (+ Direction) + 來 / 去

CHAPTER 4

Causative verbs	Subj. + 讓 / 叫 / 請 / 使 + Person + Predicate
Verbing briefly with "yixia"	Verb + 一下
Result complement "-wan" for finishing	Verb + 完 (+ 了)
Expressing "a little too" with "you yidian"	有一點 (兒) + Adj.
Conceding with "ba"	……吧

CHAPTER 5

Tag questions with "bu"	……是不是 / 對不對 / 好不好?
Result complements "-dao" and "-jian"	Verb + 到 / 見
Expressing actions in progress with "zai"	(正) 在 + Verb

CHAPTER 6

Direction complement "-qilai"	Verb / Adj.+ 起來
Expressing "everything" with "shenme dou"	什麼 + 都 / 也……

CHAPTER 7

Basic comparisons with "yiyang"	Noun 1 + 跟 / 和 + Noun 2 + 一樣 + Adj.

CHAPTER 8

Expressing "excessively" with "tai"	太 + Adj. + 了

CHAPTER 9

Expressing "will" with "hui"	會 + Verb

Credits

Story Authors : John Pasden, Jared Turner
Editor-in-Chief : John Pasden
Content Editor : Chen Shishuang
Editors : Li Jiong, Ma Lihua
Illustrator : Hu Sheng
Producer : Jared Turner

Acknowledgments

We are grateful to Ma Lihua, Li Jiong, Song Shen, Tan Rong, Chen Shishuang, and the entire team at AllSet Learning for working on this project and contributing the perfect mix of talent to produce this series.

Special thanks to Wang Hui and her 7th grade Chinese dual immersion class at Adele C. Young Intermediate School for being our test readers: AJ Bushnell, Brandon Murray, Colin Grunander, Emma Page, Isaak Diehl, Jackson Faerber, Jason Lee, Kyden Cefalo, Max Norton, Maxwell Isaacson, Olivia Barker, and Xavier Putnam. Also thanks to Jake Liu, Paris Yamamoto, Rory O'Neill, and Miles Turner for being our test readers.

About Mandarin Companion

Mandarin Companion was started by Jared Turner and John Pasden, who met one fateful day on a bus in Shanghai when the only remaining seats forced them to sit next to each other.

John majored in Japanese in college in the US and later learned Mandarin before moving to China, where he was admitted into an all-Chinese masters program in applied linguistics at East China Normal University in Shanghai. John lives in Shanghai with his wife and children. John is the editor-in-chief at Mandarin Companion and ensures each story is written at the appropriate level.

Jared decided to move to China with his young family in search of career opportunities, despite having no Chinese language skills. When he learned about Extensive Reading and started using graded readers, his language skills exploded. In 3 months, he had read 10 graded readers and quickly became conversational in Chinese. Jared lives in the US with his wife and children. Jared runs the business operations and focuses on bringing stories to life.

John and Jared work with Chinese learners and teachers all over the world. They host a podcast, You Can Learn Chinese, where they discuss the struggles and joys of learning to speak the language. They are active on social media, where they share memes and stories about learning Chinese.

You can connect with them through the website
www.mandarincompanion.com

Other Stories from Mandarin Companion

Breakthrough Readers: 150 Characters

The Misadventures of Zhou Haisheng
《周海生》
by John Pasden, Jared Turner

My Teacher Is a Martian
《我的老師是火星人》
by John Pasden, Jared Turner

Xiao Ming, Boy Sherlock
《小明》
by John Pasden, Jared Turner

Just Friends?
《我們是朋友嗎?》
by John Pasden, Jared Turner

Level 1 Readers: 300 Characters

The Secret Garden
《秘密花園》
by Frances Hodgson Burnett

The Sixty Year Dream
《六十年的夢》
by Washington Irving

The Monkey's Paw
《猴爪》
by W. W. Jacobs

The Country of the Blind
《盲人國》
by H. G. Wells

Sherlock Holmes and the Case of the Curly-Haired Company
《捲髮公司的案子》
by Sir Arthur Conan Doyle

The Prince and the Pauper
《王子和窮孩子》
by Mark Twain

Emma
《安末》
by Jane Austen

The Ransom of Red Chief
《紅猴的價格》
by O. Henry

Level 2 Readers: 450 Characters

Great Expectations: Part 1
《美好的前途（上）》
by Charles Dickens

Great Expectations: Part 2
《美好的前途（下）》
by Charles Dickens

Journey to the Center of the Earth
《地心遊記》
by Jules Verne

Jekyll and Hyde
《江可和黑德》
by Robert Louis Stevenson

Mandarin companion is producing a growing library of graded readers for Chinese language learners.

Visit our website for the newest books available:
WWW.MANDARINCOMPANION.COM

www.ingramcontent.com/pod-product-compliance
Lightning Source LLC
Chambersburg PA
CBHW050249040625
27687CB00030B/794